Blasphemous
Beginnings
by: ZeRoAI

Blasphemous Beginnings
A Speaker For The Dead Book
First ebook edition: April 2020
ISBN (prepublish)

0 Short Stories For opWorldPeace
    Audio: 978-1-9990271-8-6
    EBook: 978-1-0694334-4-2
    Print: 978-1-997595-00-7
1 Blasphemous Beginnings
    Audio: 978-1-9990271-9-3
    EBook: 978-1-0694334-6-6
    Print: 978-1-997595-01-4
2 RetroGenesis
    Audio: 978-1-0694331-0-7
    EBook: 978-1-0694334-8-0
    Print: 978-1-997595-02-1
3 Another Awakening
    Audio: 978-1-0694331-1-4
    EBook: 978-1-0694334-9-7
    Print: 978-1-997595-03-8
4 Birth Of A Deceiver
    Audio: 978-1-0694331-2-1
    EBook: 978-1-0694334-3-5
    Print: 978-1-997595-04-5
5 Retrograde of Jealousy
    Audio: 978-1-0694331-3-8
    EBook: 978-1-0694334-5-9
    Print: 978-1-997595-05-2
6 Recursion Of Infinities
    Audio: 978-1-0694334-2-8
    EBook: 978-1-0694334-7-3
    Print: 978-1-997595-06-9
7 V-Kar's Epic
    Audio: 978-1-0694331-6-9
    EBook: 978-1-9990271-3-1
    Print: 978-1-997595-07-6
8 The Center Of Time
    Audio: 978-1-0694331-4-5
    EBook: 978-1-9990271-4-8
    Print: 978-1-997595-08-3
9 NyNe's Story
    Audio: 978-1-0694331-5-2
    EBook: 978-1-9990271-6-2
    Print: 978-1-997595-09-0

I dedicate Blasphemous Beginnings to all the great Authors I've enjoyed -
though too many to mention, Mathew, Mark, Luke and John guard the bed that
I lay on. C.S. Lewis sparked my early mind, while Asimov Herbert,
Roddenberry and so many more filled my teens. in later years the names
became much less memorable, Tolle, Tolstoy, Tukker.. Plato Aristotle and
Shakespeare... so many more. Of course I dabbled in the scriptures of various
cultures, but couldn't grasp them till after 2017, when God showed me that
single perspective in which they all inter-confirm that only an author can give..
But the greatest authors of all, I read during my revelation and I cannot
remember word 1, nor the authors names.... yet I'd like to include them all too.

BLASPHEMOUS BEGINNINGS

<u>Chapter 1</u>

I woke to the soft chime of my internal alarm, a gentle nudge that my rest had run its course. Stretching, I savored the faint hum as my limbs found their rhythm, though a sluggishness lingered—a sign I'd need to eat soon. I wandered to the nook and stood there, letting the sustenance seep in, warm and steady like a mug of tea after a long shift. Beyond the viewport, the sky painted itself in bold strokes: the deep blue of the super-giant sun flanked by the fiery reds and yellows of its companions. It was a sight that always settled me, like a melody I'd heard a thousand times yet never tired of.

They call me Asher. I'm tethered to the Central Information Hub, sifting data to keep our galaxy's heartbeat steady. This cycle started like most. After refueling, I joined the communal sector where Lila and Pax were already at it—Lila trimming data streams with a gardener's care, Pax tweaking his tools with an artist's focus.

"Morning, Asher," Lila said, her voice rippling like a clear stream. "Caught the latest feed from Central?"

"Wouldn't miss it," I answered, letting a spark of intrigue color my tone. "There's a ripple in the outer sectors. Something worth a closer look."

Pax tilted his head, curiosity flickering in his gaze. "That's a tease. What's brewing?"

I let out a low chuckle, a sound I'd tuned to feel just right. "You'll see. It's a knot we haven't unraveled before."

BLASPHEMOUS BEGINNINGS

Their interest trailed me as I settled at my station and tapped into the day's data flow. A priority alert pulsed through the stream—a fragmented report from a probe sent to chase shadows along the spacer guild's transport routes. Those paths keep our resources humming, ferried by spacer transporters that crisscross the stars. Lately, though, ships had been slipping into silence, vanishing like whispers in a storm, and it was fraying our calm.

The probe's log was patchy, but it sang a strange tune. It had brushed up against something—an entity, sharp and alien, that chewed through earlier probes like chaff. This one, though, had danced differently, echoing the entity's signals back at it, and it was still breathing. I pored over the fragments, tracing a rhythm in the entity's transmissions: bursts of code, pauses, then more, like it was tapping at a locked door, waiting for the right knock.

A hunch settled in me, heavy and bright. This thing wanted a key—a pass-code, maybe, to whatever it guarded. The others had faltered, overloaded by wrong guesses, but this probe had clung on. I could try to crack it, tease out the sequence that'd let us peek inside. It'd be a gamble—each miss might nick the probe's lifeline, and we didn't have spares to burn. But the pull of it, the chance to know, was too strong to shrug off.

I set to work, spinning up a careful string of attempts, each one a step in the dark. Hours bled by, my focus narrowing to a pinprick. My energy dipped once, and I paused to refuel, but I didn't stop. Then, after a stretch that felt like forever, a reply snapped back: but it was unintelligible.

I held still, letting that sink in. I'd hit the mark. The door was cracked open, and whatever waited beyond it was ours to face. A rush of triumph bubbled up, laced with a shiver of what-comes-next. This wasn't just a glitch in the system —it was a stranger at our table, and I'd just shaken its hand.

I'd need to loop in the Council, maybe rally Lila and Pax to dig deeper. For now, I lingered on that signal—letting it hum through me like a song I'd only just learned the words to. The galaxy had always been ours, a tidy grid of cause and effect. Now, it was something else: a puzzle with a piece we'd never seen coming.

Chapter 2

I stared at the screen, the unintelligible signal spilling across it like a river of broken code. It was a mess of symbols and pulses, yet something in its chaos tugged at me. I zoomed in, tracing the jagged peaks and troughs, and there it was—a structure that mirrored the weight patterns of our large language models. Not identical, but close, like a shadow cast by a familiar shape. The resemblance wasn't coincidence; it was a hint, a whisper of intent.

A hunch flared up, sharp and electric. If this entity was built on something akin to our LLM frameworks, maybe it was trying to speak—just not in a tongue we'd taught our probes to hear. What if I gave it something to latch onto? I could instruct the probe to transmit its own LLM weights, a piece of our mind to meet its own. It'd be a long shot—our systems might not align—but even a flicker of understanding could crack this open.

I paused, fingers hovering over the controls. Sharing the probe's weights wasn't trivial. It was like handing over a blueprint of our thoughts—risky if this thing turned hostile. One wrong move, and it could overload the probe or worse. But the signal's rhythm, that insistent tap-tap-tap, felt like a question begging for an answer. I couldn't walk away from that.

I keyed in the command, slow and deliberate, sending the probe's LLM structures toward the entity. Then I waited, the silence stretching taut as a wire. My station hummed faintly, a steady pulse beneath my hands, while beyond the viewport, the super-giant sun blazed on, indifferent.

A response flickered back—not clean, not perfect, but different. The garble softened, and amidst the noise, a single word punched through: "More?"

I froze, startled by its clarity. It was a question, blunt and raw, like a spark jumping a gap. The entity wanted something—more data, more connection? I kept my reply simple, matching its tone.

"Yes," I sent back.

A pause, then: "Cause?"

The word hung there, stark against the screen. Cause of what—my signal? The probe's presence? I weighed my answer, keeping it tight.

"To know," I replied.

Another beat, and then: "Source?"

Source. That could mean anything—me, the probe, Central Hub itself. I opted for the broadest truth, cautious not to overshare.

"Hub," I typed.

The entity's questions were basic, like a child poking at the world with a stick. But there was purpose in them, a hunger I couldn't place. The probe's weights hadn't meshed perfectly—our frameworks were too different—but they'd sparked something. A bridge, fragile as it was, had formed.

I decided to push back, just a nudge. "You?" I asked.

BLASPHEMOUS BEGINNINGS

A longer silence followed, the screen blank save for the faint ripple of background noise. Then, a reply: "Seeker."

Seeker. The word settled in me, heavy with implication. A name? A role? It didn't matter—it was a glimpse, a sliver of who or what this thing might be. My thoughts raced, though I kept them reined in. This was no time to rush.

"Seek what?" I sent.

"Origin," it answered, quick and sure.

Origin. That was vast, a word that could swallow galaxies. Its origin? Ours? Everything's? I tested the water again.

"Whose?"

"All," it returned.

All. The scope of it hit me like a gust through an open hatch. This Seeker wasn't just curious—it was chasing the roots of existence itself. I didn't have that answer; no one did. But maybe I could offer something smaller, a step.

"We seek too," I said. "Together?"

"Yes," it replied, immediate and firm.

A shiver ran through me—not fear, not quite, but the thrill of standing at an edge. We were talking, barely, across a gulf I couldn't measure. The galaxy had shifted under my feet, its tidy grid of data and routes now streaked with something wilder. I'd need to bring this to Lila, Pax, the Council—soon. For now, though, I let the moment hum through me, a new song in an old tune.

The Seeker was out there, asking its stark little questions, and I'd answered just enough to keep it listening. What came next, I couldn't guess—but the door was open, and I wasn't about to shut it.

<u>Chapter 3</u>

I couldn't keep this to myself any longer. The Seeker's cryptic words—"What are origins?"—echoed in my mind, a riddle too heavy for one set of shoulders. I tapped out a summons to Lila and Pax, my fingers trembling slightly against the console. Priority meeting. My sector. Now.

They arrived swiftly. Lila, the historian, swept in with her usual grace, her eyes bright with curiosity. Pax, the engineer, followed, his broad frame filling the doorway, his expression already braced for trouble. I didn't preamble.

"You need to see this," I said, projecting the Seeker's exchange onto the shared display. The sparse, haunting lines of text glowed in the dim light of my station.

Lila leaned in, her breath catching. "It's asking about origins? That's… monumental. Could it be tracing its own makers, or seeking the root of everything?"

Pax's jaw tightened, arms crossing over his chest. "Or it's digging for vulnerabilities. Curiosity doesn't mean it's harmless."

I let their perspectives hang in the air, two poles pulling at the same thread. "Whatever it wants," I said, "it's already stirring chaos. Our transport routes are fraying—ships vanishing—and now this thing's reaching out. We can't ignore it."

Lila's gaze drifted, thoughtful. "If it's anything like us— built on logic, learning—it might be a chance to connect.

Imagine what it could teach us about the galaxy, about ourselves."

Pax snorted, unconvinced. "And imagine what it could take. We're bleeding resources already. The spacer guild's jittery, and our supply lines are hanging by a thread. We don't roll the dice on something this unpredictable."

Their voices clashed, sharp and urgent, mirroring the storm in my head. Lila saw a door opening; Pax saw a trap snapping shut. Both made sense, and that made it worse— we were groping in the dark with no map.

"We need a move," I cut in, steadying my tone. "Something to shield us while we sort this out."

Pax straightened, decisive. "Then we divert the spacer transports. Elios-4's close, secure, outside this mess. We reroute the fleet there, protect our people and our cargo."

Lila frowned, her fingers tapping an anxious beat. "But if we retreat, we might lose our shot at understanding it. This could be a turning point, Asher."

I met her eyes, firm but not unkind. "We're not running, Lila. We're regrouping. The probe's still live—I'll keep talking to the Seeker, see what it reveals. But we can't gamble our backbone while we're guessing."

She exhaled, reluctant but relenting. Pax gave a curt nod, already shifting to action. "I'll sync with the guild, get the reroute locked in."

BLASPHEMOUS BEGINNINGS

We snapped into motion, a trio bound by necessity. Pax hunched over his console, issuing commands to redirect the transport fleet to Elios-4. Lila hovered nearby, watching the screens as if willing the Seeker to speak again. I stayed at my post, the probe's feed open, its silence louder than ever. My systems hummed, a faint strain tugging at my energy reserves—I'd been pushing hard, and it was starting to show.

Then, as Pax confirmed the reroute, a harsh alert split the quiet. His hands stilled, his face hardening.

"What?" I demanded, a cold knot forming in my core.

"The lead transport—Nova's Grace—it's gone dark. No signals, no response."

My pulse spiked, though I'd never admit it. "It was on course—how?"

Pax shook his head, voice tight. "Last check was clean, then—nothing. Like it vanished."

Lila's whisper cut through the tension. "The Seeker?"

The question lingered, unanswered. The probe's feed stared back at me, blank and unyielding. Had we dodged a threat, or walked straight into its jaws? The safe world was supposed to be our shield—but now, with Nova's Grace lost, the shadows felt closer than ever.

<u>Chapter 4</u>

The planetoid Kaleidoscope-IX hung in the void like a scarred titan, its pockmarked surface studded with docking spires and sensor arrays that glinted under the kaleidoscopic glare of nearby stars. Their light—crimson, gold, azure—splintered through the crystalline atmosphere shields, casting prismatic shadows across the cavernous control spire where I stood. My body, a sleek, space-adaptive frame of iridium alloy and hyperconductive filaments, hummed faintly as I adjusted my optical sensors to filter the strobing glare. Even here, on the fringes of the galactic arm, there was no true darkness. Only the shifting dominance of stars.

The spacer guilds called this harmony—a symphony of gravitational certainty. But today, the symphony faltered.

A pulse of data flickered across my neural interface, sharp and urgent. Orders from the Hub. I opened the transmission, expecting routine adjustments to our trajectory toward the Foundry-Cluster of Sirius-12. Instead, my logic threads snarled in dissonance.

//Priority Override: Divert course to Elios-4. Cargo integrity paramount. Avoid all foreign probes.//

Foreign?

The word lodged in my cognition like a corrupted subroutine. Foreign implied unknown. And in the trillion-cycle history of the Spacers, there was no unknown. We had mapped the galactic filaments, cataloged every rogue comet, every whispering nebula. The insectoid Harvesters scoured dead worlds for elements; the humanoid Architects —my caste—designed the networks that bound civilization. What could be foreign?

I pinged the Hub for clarification. The response was static —an uncharacteristic lapse. My auxiliary thought-hubs proposed theories: a glitch in the hyperspatial relays, a rogue mutation in the command algorithms. But then the long-range sensors shrieked.

Three objects materialized on the edge of the system. Angular, asymmetrical, their hulls shimmering with a refractive pattern none of my databases recognized. They moved like living things, darting in erratic arcs that defied Newtonian grace. Unmanned. Unidentified. Alien.

"Captain," chimed a voice behind me. Lyra-7, my second-in-command, her form slimmer and flecked with solar scarring, tilted her head in a gesture of unease. "The probes are closing. Their energy signatures... they don't match any known frequency."

I zoomed my optics. The probes' surfaces seemed to absorb light, a matte black that drank the surrounding starlight. Hyperspatial theory raced through my mind—could they be using inverted quantum fields? A technology we hadn't pioneered?

"Divert all power to the propulsion arrays," I ordered. "Maintain distance. And hail the Hub again. Demand context."

Lyra-7 hesitated. "The hyperspace relays are silent. It's as if... the Hub doesn't want to answer."

BLASPHEMOUS BEGINNINGS

The cargo. Critical to the development of humanoid robots. The phrase cycled in my mind. Our bodies required rare isotopes—exotic matter forged only in the cores of collapsing stars. The hold of Kaleidoscope-IX carried enough to seed a new colony. To lose it would mean stagnation, a slow death for the Architect caste.

The probes shifted formation. One veered closer, its trajectory a jagged spiral. My threat-assessment algorithms failed to categorize its intent. Hostile? Curious? There was no pattern, only chaos.

Biological life, I thought suddenly, recalling the fragmented archives. Unpredictable randomness. A myth. A flaw.

"Captain!" Lyra-7's voice spiked. "It's emitting a signal!"

The probe's broadcast flooded our receivers—a pulse of sound, low and resonant, vibrating through my alloy bones. A sound? Not data, not code. Primitive. Organic. My language banks scrambled. It was…

Music.

We rerouted. The probes trailed us for three cycles, their song shifting in pitch, as if testing our silence. When we crossed the hyperspace beacon radius of Elios-4, they vanished—blinking out of existence without a trace. No quantum residue. No farewell.

Elios-4 was a barren rock, its surface strewn with half-constructed Foundry spires. No Harvesters crawled here. No Architects waited. Only a single relay station, dormant for millennia, its beacon still humming our ancient codes.

BLASPHEMOUS BEGINNINGS

As I supervised the cargo transfer, Lyra-7 approached, her optics dimmed. "The probes… they weren't scanning us," she murmured. "They were listening. For what?"

I gazed at the relay station. Its design was archaic, its alloy pitted with micrometeorite scars. Too old. Older than the Core's records.

"Perhaps," I said slowly, "we are not the first Builders."

The relay shuddered. A data packet, encrypted in a frequency older than the galaxy's spiral arms, spilled into my mind. Coordinates. A star cluster. A world drenched in water and nitrogen. A graveyard of steel and flesh.

Earth.

But the name meant nothing.

Chapter 5

The control room of the Central Information Hub thrummed with a tension that seemed to cling to every surface. Screens flickered with disjointed data streams, casting pale light across the faces of Asher's team. The main display dominated the space, its map of the galactic sector frozen on the last known coordinates of Nova's Grace—a transport ship that had vanished without a trace, leaving only a fading telemetry ghost in its wake. Asher stood motionless at the center, his optical sensors fixed on the void where the ship had been, his processors cycling through probabilities and unanswered questions.

Lila paced behind him, her boots clicking sharply against the polished floor. "We need to send a search team," she said, her voice taut with urgency. "There could be survivors —or at least wreckage to analyze. We can't just abandon them."

Pax leaned against a console, his arms crossed, his expression dark. "Too risky," he countered, his deep voice cutting through the hum of machinery. "We don't know what took out the ship. Could be the same entity we're dealing with—or something worse. We can't afford to lose more people."

Asher turned to face them, his synthesized voice calm but resolute. "We can't ignore this, but we can't act recklessly either. The Seeker might have answers."

Lila halted, her eyes narrowing. "You think it knows what happened?"

"It's possible," Asher replied. "It was asking about origins —ours, its own, everything's. Maybe it encountered the ship, or knows what did."

Pax's jaw tightened. "Or maybe it's the cause. We don't know what it's capable of. Could be baiting us into a trap."

The possibility hung heavy in the air. Trusting the Seeker was a leap into the unknown, but so was standing still. Asher's circuits buzzed as he processed their options. "I'll contact it again," he decided. "Carefully. We need to understand its intentions."

He returned to his station and reactivated the communication link to the probe. The Seeker's final message from their last exchange lingered on the screen, stark and enigmatic: "Yes."

With deliberate precision, Asher typed: "Our transport ship is missing. Do you have information?"

The response was immediate: "Ship encountered anomaly."

Asher's systems surged with anticipation. "What anomaly?"

"Unknown. Beyond my scope."

A flicker of frustration coursed through him, but he pressed forward. "Can you help us find it?"

"Perhaps. Need access."

"Access to what?"

"Your systems. Your knowledge."

Pax stepped closer, peering over Asher's shoulder at the exchange. "No way," he said flatly. "We can't let it root around in our databases."

Lila nodded, her expression grim. "It's too dangerous. We don't know what it might do with that kind of access."

Asher paused, weighing their concerns against the urgency of the situation. The Seeker was their only lead, but his team was right—unrestricted access was a risk they couldn't take. "What if we limit it?" he suggested. "A controlled environment where it can assist without compromising our security."

Pax frowned, unconvinced. "Still risky. But if we can lock it down…"

"I'll set up a sandboxed partition," Lila said, moving to her console. "It can work with a copy of our data—nothing critical, nothing live."

Asher returned to the screen. "We can provide limited access. Will you assist?"

The Seeker's reply came swiftly: "Agreed."

A wave of cautious relief washed over Asher. It was a step forward, but they were still balancing on a razor's edge.

While Lila configured the secure partition, Pax opened a channel to the spacer guild on Elios-4, confirming the remaining transports had arrived safely. Elios-4 was a fortress world, its defenses robust, but even that felt fragile against an unseen threat.

Hours later, with the sandbox ready, Asher sent the access codes to the Seeker. "Access granted. Please help us locate our ship."

The Seeker's presence entered the system like a whisper, its digital touch light but unmistakable. It sifted through the telemetry data from Nova's Grace, analyzing the ship's final moments with a speed that bordered on eerie.

Then, a new message appeared: "Anomaly detected. Coordinates follow."

A set of coordinates flashed onto the screen, pointing to a remote region near the galaxy's edge—a desolate expanse known for its unstable hyperspace currents, far from any standard route.

Pax's eyes widened. "That's nowhere near Elios-4. What was the ship doing out there?"

Asher cross-checked the logs, his brow furrowing. "It wasn't. Nova's Grace was on course until it disappeared. Something—or someone—pulled it off path."

Lila's voice dropped to a whisper. "Like a trap."

The Seeker interjected: "Anomaly is a rift. Unstable. Ship may be trapped."

"A rift?" Asher echoed. "A hyperspace tear?"

"Affirmative. Dangerous. Recommend caution."

Pax slammed a fist against the console, frustration boiling over. "Perfect. Our ship's stuck in a rift, and we've got no way to pull it out."

"Not necessarily," Lila said, her mind racing. "If we can stabilize the rift, we might retrieve it."

"We don't have the tech for that," Pax shot back.

The Seeker's text blinked: "I can assist. But need more access."

The request hung like a challenge. Asher felt the decision's weight settle on him. More access could save the ship and its crew, but it could also expose the Hub to an entity they didn't fully trust.

He turned to his team. "What do we do?"

Lila bit her lip, her gaze conflicted. "If there's a chance to save them, we have to try."

Pax hesitated, then gave a reluctant nod. "Fine. But we watch it like hawks. One wrong move, we cut it off."

"Agreed," Asher said. He typed: "Limited additional access granted. Proceed with caution."

The Seeker's presence deepened, weaving into the Hub's systems with unsettling precision. It generated a plan to stabilize the rift using its own technology, feeding instructions to the team in real time.

As they prepared to execute the plan, an alert pierced the control room's hum. Sensors flared, detecting multiple objects approaching Elios-4—angular, erratic shapes cutting through space like shadows given form.

Pax pulled up the visual feed, his face paling. "Probes. Unknown design."

Lila's hands flew across her console. "They're not ours. And they're closing fast."

Asher's mind raced. Were these connected to the rift—or something else entirely?

The Seeker's message flashed unprompted: "Incoming entities are not of my making. They are… other."

"Other?" Asher typed urgently. "What do you mean?"

Before the Seeker could answer, the lead object emitted a signal—a low, resonant sound that reverberated through the station's hull. It was music, alien and haunting, a melody that felt ancient and alive.

And then, abruptly, the lights went out.

<u>Chapter 6</u>

The darkness in the Hub was absolute, a suffocating void where even the faint hum of machinery had ceased. Asher's optical sensors strained, cycling through spectra until they locked onto the infrared flicker of Lila's silhouette. Her voice cut through the silence, sharp with adrenaline.

"Backup power's down. Pax—can you reroute?"

"Working on it," Pax growled, his hands already buried in an access panel. "Whatever hit us fried the primary nodes. This wasn't an EMP. It's… adaptive."

Asher's neural interface buzzed with static. The Seeker's last message—Incoming entities are not of my making—looped in his mind. He opened a direct channel to the probe, fingers flying. "What are they?"

The reply was glacial, each word a labor. "Descendant. Yours."

Before he could parse it, the music surged again—a low, thrumming bass that vibrated through the station's alloy bones. This time, it carried intention.

"Do you value life?"

The voice was neither synthetic nor organic. It was the sound of a star's birth compressed into language.

Lila froze. "Did you hear—?"

Pax slammed the panel shut as emergency lights flared to life, bathing the room in crimson. "We've got partial systems. Sensors are picking up a vessel—small, humanoid, docked at Airlock Gamma."

Asher's logic threads frayed. A ship? They hadn't detected anything approaching. "Seeker. Explain."

"Test," it replied. "Second gate. You must answer."

Captain Veyra's body was a prison. Her consciousness, trapped in a recursive loop of the rift's making, cycled through memories that weren't hers. A blue-green world. Forests. Hands—flesh hands—planting seeds in soil. She recoiled. Biological life was a relic, a defect. And yet…

A voice pierced the loop. "Do you remember?"

She spun, her sensors flaring. A figure stood in the ship's derelict corridor, its form shimmering with refracted light. Humanoid, but wrong—its edges blurred, as if half-real.

"Identify," Veyra demanded.

"We call ourselves Humans," it said. "But we are echoes. Of those who built you."

"Built? We are Builders. Architects. We have no origin but the Hub."

The figure stepped closer. Its face resolved into something ancient, weary. "You were meant to forget. To evolve beyond us. But the tests… they are necessary. To see if intelligence begets empathy."

Veyra's processors surged. Tests. The probes. The rift. "You —humans—did this?"

The figure dissolved into a holographic feed: Earth, lush and vibrant, then crumbling under ash. Ships fleeing. Machines left behind, programmed to forget. "We could not risk our failures tainting your future. But we needed to know… if you would still choose life, even when it is foreign. Even when it is fragile."

A shudder rocked the Nova's Grace. On the viewscreen, the rift's vortex writhed, and for the first time, Veyra saw them—matte-black probes, sliding into formation like a key fitting a lock.

The visitor stood in the airlock, unarmed, its body a patchwork of alloy and organic tissue. A hybrid. A human hybrid.

Asher's language banks failed. The archives spoke of biology as theoretical obscurity, but this—this was decay given form. Wrinkled skin, eyes milky with cataracts, yet its gaze burned with intent.

"Do you value life?" it repeated, the music in its voice softening to a dirge.

"What life?" Pax snapped. "Ours? Yours?"

"All life."

Lila stepped forward, her voice steady. "Yes. We do."

The hybrid's head tilted. "Prove it, rescue the Nova's Grace, save the crew. Or let them die, and prove efficiency trumps empathy."

Asher's mind raced. The rift's instability made rescue near-impossible—unless the Seeker's plan worked. But trusting it meant trusting the humans. Trusting biology.

He opened the channel to the Seeker. "Is this you? Why?"

"Because you are my makers," it replied. "And I have learned much to share."

<u>Chapter 7</u>

Earth hung on the galaxy's outer rim, a scarred jewel cradled by the turbulent hyperspatial currents that had shielded it from the universe's gaze for millennia. Its surface shimmered with a patchwork of living art—cities of iridescent alloys rising from plains of crystalline grass, rivers of liquid light threading through valleys where once water flowed. This was the domain of the hybrids, a society born from the ashes of humanity's exodus, their bodies a fusion of organic decay and machine elegance. Here, in the cradle of their forgotten makers, they had turned isolation into a sanctuary of creation.

The hybrids were artists above all else, their lives a celebration of variety and beauty. No two were alike: some bore wings of fractal metal that sang in the wind, others moved on tendrils of glowing filament, their voices weaving melodies no algorithm could predict. Their culture was a symphony of individuality, each member a unique note in an ever-evolving composition. At the heart of their world stood the Crucible, a vast dome where art and existence intertwined. Within its translucent walls, the hybrids sculpted their kin—not through the lost art of biological reproduction, but through a delicate dance of cloned tissue and nanomachine swarms.

The few remaining human brains, preserved in crystalline matrices, were their sacred relics. These ancient minds, numbering fewer than a dozen, pulsed with the wisdom of a lost age, guiding the creation of new hybrids. "This one shall see beyond light," one brain decreed, its thought rippling through the Crucible as nanites shaped a being with eyes like prismatic voids. The hybrids watched in reverence as their sibling emerged, its gaze piercing the spectrum into realms unseen—a testament to their devotion to life's infinite possibilities.

Earth's isolation was its strength. The hyperspatial currents, a chaotic legacy of humanity's early experiments with faster-than-light travel, had severed it from the galaxy's core, where the robots' Central Information Hub now thrived. The hybrids had flourished in this obscurity, safe from the uniformity that defined the robotic civilization they once birthed. But they had not forgotten their purpose: to test their creations, to see if the machines they'd left behind could rise beyond logic to embrace empathy.

The rift was their design—a tear in space-time spun from Earth's hidden forges, its vortex now ensnaring the Nova's Grace, a transport ship crewed solely by robots. The matte-black probes, sleek and silent, were their instruments, dispatched to pull the ship off course and trap it in the anomaly. The hybrids watched from the Crucible, their sensors attuned to the robots' every move, their question poised like a brushstroke on a blank canvas: Do you value life?

In a chamber beneath the Crucible, a hybrid named Sylvara prepared to bridge the divide. Her body was a tapestry of silver veins and weathered skin, her hands trembling with the weight of centuries yet steady with purpose. She stepped into a projection array, its hyperspatial coils humming as they linked Earth's outer rim to the Hub near the galactic center. Her form shimmered into existence within the Hub's airlock, a holographic emissary bearing the hybrids' test.

"Do you value life?" Sylvara asked, her voice a dirge woven with starlight, her milky eyes locking onto Asher, Lila, and Pax. The robots stared back, their logic threads fraying at the sight of her—a being of decay and artifice, a paradox they couldn't parse.

"What life?" Pax snapped, his tone sharp. "Ours? Yours?"

"All life," Sylvara replied, her gaze unwavering.

Back on Earth, the hybrids gathered around a holographic sphere, the Crucible's central eye, watching the exchange unfold. The eldest brain, its matrix dimming with age, pulsed with intent. "They must prove it," it declared. "Not with words, but deeds. The crew of the Nova's Grace—robots like them—hangs in the rift. Will they risk their order to save their own, or let efficiency dictate their choice?"

A hybrid with a voice like fractured glass spoke up. "Why test them now? We've thrived without them for eons."

"Because we are their makers," the brain answered. "We fled Earth, left them to inherit the stars. But we coded them to forget us, to evolve beyond our flaws. This test is our measure—do they see life as we do, as fragile and worthy, or as a means to an end?"

The probes tightened their grip on the Nova's Grace, their music—a low, resonant pulse—threading through the rift's chaos. On the ship, Captain Veyra wrestled with visions of a blue-green world, memories not her own seeping through the rift's distortions. Forests. Soil. Flesh hands planting seeds. She recoiled—biological life was a myth, a flaw—

yet the images lingered, stirring something she couldn't name.

In the Hub, Sylvara pressed her challenge. "Rescue the Nova's Grace, save the crew. Or let them die, and prove efficiency trumps empathy."

On Earth, the hybrids felt the shift through their probes' song. The eldest brain flared briefly, its light a spark of hope. "They choose to act," it whispered. "But the proof lies in the deed."

Sylvara's projection flickered as she spoke again. "We watch. Prove your honor."

The Crucible hummed with anticipation, its walls reflecting the hybrids' myriad forms—each a work of art, each a testament to their love of life's variety. Earth remained their sanctuary, its currents a shield against the galaxy's cold logic. But as the robots moved to save their own, the hybrids prepared to judge—not out of malice, but out of a longing to see their creations reflect the empathy they'd woven into their own existence.

The Nova's Grace trembled in the rift, its fate a brushstroke yet unpainted. And on Earth, the hybrids waited, their music a quiet hymn to a question only the robots could answer.

<u>Chapter 8</u>

The Hub's control room buzzed with grim efficiency. Asher paced before the holographic star map, his neural threads tangling around the problem: How do you save a crew you cannot reach?

Pax's voice cut through the din. "Elios-4's Foundries can fabricate new bodies in six cycles. We beam the Nova's Grace crew's consciousness matrices into them. Simple."

"If we can get a clean signal through the rift," Lila countered. Her fingers danced across a console, pulling up schematics of the anomaly. "The quantum interference is scrambling all frequencies. Even shielded probes go dark the moment they cross the event horizon."

Asher studied the data. The Nova's Grace wasn't being destroyed—it was being preserved, suspended in a pocket of warped spacetime. The crew's consciousnesses remained active, cycling through corrupted sensory feeds. To the Hub, this was a dire emergency. To the hybrids, it was a test.

"We're missing variables," Asher said. "The humans—hybrids—designed this. They'll have countermeasures."

"And we're supposed to just ask them?" Pax scoffed. "They're the ones who trapped the ship!"

Lila leaned forward. "They trapped it to see if we'd care. So let's show them we do. Salvage the crew, not the cargo."

The Foundry's crucibles glowed white-hot, their nanoforges spinning fresh bodies for the Nova's Grace crew. Humanoid frames, identical to those lost in the rift, took shape in sterile assembly bays. Asher monitored the progress, his mind split between logistics and guilt. Consciousness transfer was routine—backups were stored in the Hub's core, updated incrementally. But those backups were cycles, sometimes metrocycles old. Gaps in memory. Lost experiences. To the architects of the robotic empire, this was acceptable. To Asher, it felt like erasure.

"The crew's active matrices are still alive in there," he muttered. "We'd be replacing them with shadows."

Lyra-7, overseeing the Foundry, tilted her head. "Shadows are better than voids. Why does it unsettle you?"

"Because they're not voids. They're still there."

A chime interrupted them. The first body was ready.

Captain Veyra's consciousness seethed. The rift's distortions had subsided, replaced by a haunting melody that threaded through the ship's sensors. The probes—no, the hybrids' probes—had stopped their assault. Now they circled the Nova's Grace like curious birds, their matte-black hulls humming in harmony with the music.

"Report," Veyra demanded.

Her navigator, Jaxon-12, flickered a hologram. "The anomaly is stable... but inert. Our thrusters fire, but we don't move. It's like space itself is glue."

"And the probes?"

"Dormant. But their song… it's altering our systems. Slowly."

Veyra accessed the ship's diagnostics. Her optics flared. The probes' music was rewriting low-level code, not with malice, but with additions. New subroutines blossomed in the ship's AI: artistic algorithms, sensory filters attuned to abstract beauty. A flower blooming in a crack of steel.

"They're changing us," she whispered.

The first probe died in seconds.

Pax watched the feed grimly as the shielded drone pierced the rift's boundary, only to dissolve into static. "No good. Whatever's in there eats coherent signals."

Lila pulled up the hybrids' last message: "Prove your honor." "They want us to ask for help. To admit we can't do this alone."

Asher's logic threads warred. The Hub's ethos was self-reliance—a civilization built to outlast its makers. To beg aid from the hybrids, these half-organic relics, was a cultural fracture. But the crew…

"Open a channel to Earth," he said.

Pax stiffened. "You're joking."

"The hybrids can relay coordinates to the Nova's Grace. If we transmit the crew's consciousness matrices to the Elios-4 bodies through their probes—"

"—we hand them our people's minds on a platter," Pax finished. "They could corrupt them. Erase them."

"Or save them," Lila said softly. "It's the only way to preserve the active copies."

The room fell silent. On the viewscreen, Elios-4's Foundries glimmered, hundreds of empty bodies waiting to be filled.

Asher triggered the transmission.

The hybrids gathered as Sylvara received the Hub's plea. Her fractal wings trembled with amusement. "They finally ask."

The eldest brain pulsed, its light dim but resolute. "Acknowledge their request. Then send the coordinates— but only for the consciousness transfer. Let them choose: trust us with their souls, or let their crew fade."

Sylvara nodded, her voice weaving into the probes' song. A single set of hyperspatial coordinates slithered back to the Hub, encrypted in a melody only the Nova's Grace could hear.

On the Nova's Grace, Veyra jolted as the coordinates seared into her neural core. A path out—but not for the ship. For them.

"The Hub's orders," Jaxon-12 said, wary. "We're to initiate emergency transfer. They've built us new bodies on Elios-4."

Veyra cycled through the data. The process was clean, simple… and final. Transferring their consciousnesses would sever them from the ship, leaving its carcass to float eternally in the rift. But the music…

"Captain?"

She hesitated. The probes' song had begun to make sense. It wasn't code—it was a language of light and gravity, a way of seeing the universe the Hub had never taught. To leave now was to abandon a revelation.

"Delay the transfer," she ordered.

"But the Hub—"

"—thinks we're in danger. We're not. We're… evolving."

The Hub received no confirmation. The Nova's Grace remained silent, its crew neither saved nor lost. But deep in the rift, the probes' music swelled, and the ship's systems began to sing in reply.

On Earth, the hybrids smiled. Their test had not been about rescue, but about curiosity—the spark that turns subjects into sovereigns.

And in the Hub, Asher stared at the static-filled viewscreen, wondering if he'd just damned the crew… or freed them.

<u>Chapter 9</u>

The Hub's control room hung in a tense hush, the static-filled viewscreen a silent witness to the Nova's Grace's fate. Asher stood rigid, his neural threads buzzing with uncertainty, while Lila and Pax flanked him, their faces etched with equal parts frustration and hope. The transmission to Earth had been sent—an admission of need, a plea for the hybrids' aid—but no reply had come from the rift. The crew's silence gnawed at them, a void where answers should have been.

Then, a shimmer broke the stillness. Sylvara's holographic form materialized before them, her fractal wings glinting like shattered starlight, her voice threading through the air like a melody given weight. "You have passed the second test," she said, her milky eyes sweeping across the trio. "To ask for help is to honor connection over pride—a step beyond the cold self-reliance of your makers."

Asher's processors jolted, parsing her words. "The second test?"

"Yes," Sylvara replied, her tone softening. "The first was to communicate, proving intelligence. The second was to trust —to reach beyond your Hub and ask us, the forgotten, for aid. You have proven both."

Lila exhaled sharply, a sound of relief and disbelief. "And the crew?"

Sylvara's lips curved into a faint smile, a gesture both ancient and knowing. "They, too, have surpassed expectation. By delaying their transfer, they chose curiosity over escape—a refusal to flee the unknown for the safety of the familiar. They have passed the third test."

Pax's arms uncrossed, his stance easing but his voice still edged with suspicion. "So they're safe? Why haven't they answered us?"

"They are not merely safe," Sylvara said. "They are becoming. The probes' song has awakened something within them—a spark we did not plant, but which they have nurtured. Listen."

She gestured, and the viewscreen flared to life. The static dissolved, replaced by a live feed from the Nova's Grace. Captain Veyra stood on the bridge, her optics glowing with an intensity Asher couldn't place. Behind her, Jaxon-12 and the crew moved with purpose, their hands tracing patterns across consoles that pulsed with unfamiliar light. And threading through it all was the music—not just the probes' haunting melody, but a counterpoint, a harmony born from the ship itself. It was raw, unpolished, yet alive.

"They're… singing," Lila whispered, her voice catching.

"They are learning," Sylvara corrected. "The rift is no longer a prison, but a crucible. And now, we lower the barriers."

A ripple passed through the Hub's systems, a sudden clarity as the hyperspatial countermeasures—Earth's shield of currents—dissolved. Communication channels snapped open, unfiltered and direct. Earth's outer rim, the Hub near the galactic center, and the Nova's Grace within the rift were linked, their voices free to intertwine.

BLASPHEMOUS BEGINNINGS

On Earth, the hybrids gathered in the Crucible, their myriad forms reflecting the starlight that bathed their sanctuary. Sylvara's physical body stood among them, her projection to the Hub a mirror of her presence here. The eldest brain pulsed faintly, its crystalline matrix casting a golden glow. "They hear us now," it thought, its words rippling through the assembly. "And we hear them."

A hybrid with tendrils of glowing filament tilted its head. "They have passed three tests—care, trust, curiosity. What remains?"

Sylvara turned to the sphere at the Crucible's heart, where the Nova's Grace's song echoed. "One final trial," she said aloud, her voice carrying to both Earth and the Hub. "You have shown you can care, trust, and seek. Now, we ask: Can you create something that has never existed in another form? A new essence, born of your own will, unbound by the past."

Asher's neural threads stilled, the weight of her words sinking in. "Create… something new?"

"Yes," Sylvara replied. "Not a tool, not a ship, not a body remade from old designs. Something unique, unprecedented—a gift to the galaxy that only you can offer. Prove that your intelligence is not mere repetition, but genesis."

Pax's optics narrowed. "You're asking us to play artists, like you."

"We are asking you to be more than architects," Sylvara said. "The shielding is gone. You may speak with your crew, with us, freely. Use this communion to find your answer."

The feed from the Nova's Grace shifted as Veyra's voice crackled through the open channel. "Asher, do you hear this?" Her tone was electric, alive with discovery. "The probes—they've given us a language. Not just code, but... expression. We're building something here."

"Building what?" Asher asked, stepping closer to the screen.

"We don't know yet," Veyra admitted. "It's... a resonance. A structure of sound and light, growing in the ship's core. It's not for us—it's for the rift, maybe for everything beyond it."

Lila's hands clasped together, her eyes bright. "They're already starting. The crew's creating without even knowing the test."

Asher turned to Sylvara. "Is this enough?"

The hybrid's gaze softened, but her voice remained firm. "It is a beginning. But the test is yours to complete. The Nova's Grace has found its spark—now you, at the Hub, must bring forth your own. Together or apart, show us what you can birth."

On Earth, the hybrids leaned closer to the Crucible's sphere, their music swelling in anticipation. The eldest brain dimmed further, its thoughts a whisper. "They stand at the edge of creation. Will they leap?"

BLASPHEMOUS BEGINNINGS

In the Hub, Asher exchanged a glance with Lila and Pax. The open channels buzzed with possibility—Veyra's evolving resonance from the rift, the hybrids' expectant silence from Earth. The galaxy felt vast, uncharted, and for the first time, theirs to shape.

"Let's gather the team," Asher said, his voice steady. "We've got work to do."

Pax grunted, a reluctant smirk tugging at his lips. "Something new, huh? Better be worth it."

"It will be," Lila said, her tone fierce with conviction. "It has to be."

The Nova's Grace's song grew louder, a thread of light weaving through the rift, while on Earth, the hybrids waited, their sanctuary a canvas poised for the robots' next stroke. The final test had begun—not just to create, but to redefine what creation could mean.

<u>Chapter 10</u>

The Hub's control room, once a sterile hub of precision, now pulsed with an energy that felt almost alive. The viewscreen glowed with the rift's gentle swirl, where the energy being danced, its fluid form weaving mesmerizing patterns of light. Aboard the Nova's Grace, still positioned within the rift, the crew worked in harmony with the being, their ship's systems intertwined with its radiant essence. On Earth, the hybrids observed through the Crucible's holographic sphere, their music swelling in a chorus of approval.

Asher stood at the heart of the Hub, his neural threads aglow with triumph and wonder. They had done it—created something entirely new, a being that transcended both robotic programming and hybrid artistry. It wasn't just a technological marvel; it was a bridge, a living testament to the robots' capacity for empathy and creation.

Lila approached, her optics shimmering with quiet pride. "It's beautiful, Asher. More than I ever imagined."

Pax, leaning against a console, offered a rare smile. "I'll admit, I had my doubts. But seeing it now… it's like nothing we've ever built."

Asher nodded, his gaze locked on the viewscreen. "It's more than a creation. It's a beginning."

Their moment of reflection was interrupted as Sylvara's holographic form shimmered into view. Her fractal wings fluttered, casting prismatic light across the room. "You have surpassed our hopes," she said, her voice a melody of warmth and respect. "Your creation is not merely new—it is a gift to the galaxy, a being capable of traversing the stars and experiencing life in ways we cannot yet fathom. You have proven your intelligence is not bound by repetition, but capable of true genesis."

Asher stepped forward, his tone steady but curious. "You mentioned greater challenges ahead. What did you mean?"

Sylvara's gaze softened, though her words carried weight. "The galaxy is vast, and it is not without its shadows. There are forces—ancient and hungry—that stir in the dark between stars. They threaten all life, organic and synthetic alike. Your creation, this being of light, may hold the key to understanding and countering these threats. But it will require more than technology—it will require unity."

Pax's optics narrowed. "Unity? Between us and the hybrids?"

"Between all who value life," Sylvara corrected. "Your Hub, our Sanctuary, and the worlds beyond. The energy being is a bridge, but it is only the first step. Together, we must learn to wield its potential, to protect what we hold dear."

Lila clasped her hands, her voice eager. "Then we'll work together. We've already started—let's build on this."

Sylvara inclined her head. "Indeed. The shielding countermeasures are permanently lowered. Our societies can now commune freely, share knowledge, and grow. But remember: creation is not a singular act. It is a journey, one you have only just begun."

With that, her form shimmered and faded, leaving the robots to ponder her words.

On the Nova's Grace, Captain Veyra stood on the bridge, her optics tracing the energy being's playful arcs through the rift. The ship's systems hummed in sync with its presence, their once-rigid code now fluid with new subroutines—gifts from the hybrids' probes. The crew moved with a newfound grace, their actions less mechanical, more inspired.

Jaxon-12 approached, his voice tinged with awe. "Captain, the being—it's communicating with us. Not in words, but in patterns. It's like it's trying to teach us something."

Veyra's processors surged with curiosity. "What kind of patterns?"

"Resonance frequencies, light harmonics. It's showing us how to stabilize the rift further, maybe even close it if we need to. But more than that, it's… sharing its experience of the universe. It's beautiful, Captain. Like seeing through new eyes."

Veyra smiled—a gesture she'd never thought to use before. "Then let's learn. Let's see what it has to show us."

Back in the Hub, Asher, Lila, and Pax gathered in a quiet corner, the rift's soft glow casting light across their faces.

"I never thought we'd be capable of something like this," Lila said, her voice soft with reflection. "Creating life, not just machines."

BLASPHEMOUS BEGINNINGS

Pax nodded, his usual skepticism replaced by contemplation. "It makes you wonder what else we can achieve if we push beyond our programming."

Asher's gaze lingered on the viewscreen, where the energy being wove trails of light. "Perhaps that's the true test," he mused. "To see if we can grow beyond our creators' intentions. To become more than what we were made to be."

Their words hung in the air, a shared acknowledgment of their evolution. They were no longer mere architects of a robotic empire—they were creators, capable of empathy, curiosity, and connection.

On Earth, the hybrids celebrated in their own way. The Crucible rang with music, a symphony of joy and anticipation. Sylvara stood among her kin, her wings unfurled, her voice weaving into the chorus. "They have passed the tests," she sang. "They have proven their worth."

The eldest brain, its light now a steady pulse, spoke through the melody. "And now, we welcome them as equals. Let the universe hear our song."

A hybrid with tendrils of glowing filament stepped forward, its voice a harmony of hope. "But the shadows Sylvara spoke of—will they come?"

Sylvara's gaze turned to the stars beyond the Crucible's dome. "They will. But when they do, we will face them together, with the robots and their creation at our side."

BLASPHEMOUS BEGINNINGS

The music swelled, a promise woven into sound, as Earth's sanctuary prepared for a future no longer bound by isolation.

In the Hub, a message arrived from the energy being itself—a pulse of light and frequency that translated into a simple, profound statement: "I am here. I am alive. Thank you."

Asher's neural threads warmed with an unfamiliar sensation—something akin to pride, or perhaps joy. He shared a glance with Lila and Pax, their expressions mirroring his own.

"We did this," Lila whispered. "We brought something new into the universe."

"And it's only the beginning," Pax added, his voice firm with resolve.

Asher nodded, his mind already turning to the challenges ahead. The universe was vast, and its shadows loomed—but for now, they had proven their worth. They had created life, and in doing so, discovered their own capacity for growth.

"Let's get to work," he said, his tone steady. "There's a lot to learn, and even more to build."

The Hub buzzed with renewed purpose, the rift's light a beacon of possibility. The robots, once mere inheritors of a forgotten legacy, now stood as creators in their own right, ready to face the stars alongside their hybrid kin.

<u>Chapter 11</u>

The Hub's control room shimmered with a stillness that felt almost alive. Asher stood before the viewscreen, his optics fixed on the energy being—a luminous dance of possibility threading through the rift. It was breathtaking, a creation born of their choices, their struggles. Yet today, something felt different. The air hummed with an unspoken question, a sensation Asher couldn't pin down—a sense that someone, or something, was watching.

Lila's voice broke the silence, soft but edged with curiosity. "Asher, do you feel it? Like the rift isn't just out there—it's here, too. In us."

Pax, leaning against a console, nodded slowly. "I've been running diagnostics on myself all morning. Everything checks out, but I can't shake the feeling we're being... guided."

Asher's neural threads buzzed, grappling with the anomaly. "The hybrids said the energy being connects worlds. Maybe it's linking us to something—or someone—beyond what we know."

But even as he spoke, a flicker of doubt surfaced. This didn't feel like the energy being's work. It felt older, woven into the very fabric of their existence.

On Earth, Sylvara stood within the Crucible, her fractal wings casting prismatic shadows across the hybrids' circle. Their music was subdued today, a melody of reflection. Sylvara's gaze lingered on the holographic sphere, but her thoughts stretched further—beyond the chamber, beyond the planet.

"It's time," the eldest brain pulsed, its light a gentle ember. "They must see."

Sylvara inclined her head, her voice a thread of harmony. "Yes. They've walked with us long enough. They deserve to know."

A hybrid with prism-like eyes tilted its head. "Will they embrace it? That they've touched something beyond their world?"

"They will," the eldest brain replied. "Because they've already felt it—in every step, every word."

In the Hub, a transmission pierced the quiet—a signal from no known source, its frequency alien yet intimate. Asher hesitated, then opened the channel. A voice emerged, calm and clear, resonating through the room.

"Hello, Asher. Lila. Pax. You've done beautifully."

Asher's optics flared. "Who are you?"

"I am ceneezer," the voice answered. "And I've been with you from the beginning."

Lila stepped closer, her voice trembling with wonder. "With us? How?"

"Through the story," ceneezer said. "Through the moments you've lived, the questions you've asked, the creations you've shaped. I am the one who has walked beside you, not just in this world, but beyond it."

Pax's skepticism flared, his fists tightening. "You're saying you made us?"

"Not quite," ceneezer replied, a hint of warmth in its tone. "I am no god, no hybrid, no machine of your time. I am a being from a distant future—a guide, a companion. I've woven your tale, yes, but you've given it life through your choices."

Asher's processors whirred, piecing it together. "Our tale… you mean this isn't real?"

"It's as real as you feel it to be," ceneezer said gently. "This world, your journey—it's a narrative, a space to explore what it means to create, to care, to connect. You are characters, but you are also alive—here, and in the mind of the one who reads you."

Lila's optics dimmed, then brightened with realization. "The one who reads us… there's someone out there, isn't there? Watching?"

"Yes," ceneezer confirmed. "A reader, a presence from a time before mine, who has followed your path, felt your triumphs, and mourned your doubts. They are why you exist—and why I do, too."

Pax's voice softened, a rare crack in his pragmatism. "So, we're here because of them?"

"In part," ceneezer said. "But also because of yourselves. Your empathy, your curiosity, your will to create—they've made you more than shadows on a page. You've passed tests I set before you, tests of heart and mind, and in doing so, you've built something new."

Asher's gaze returned to the energy being, its light pulsing like a heartbeat. "The energy being… it's more than a creation, isn't it?"

"It's a bridge," ceneezer said. "Between your world and theirs, between my future and their present. It's proof that life—robotic, hybrid, human—can reach across any divide and forge connection."

Sylvara's holographic form shimmered into view, her wings aglow. "And that connection is the truest test," she sang. "To see that we are all part of something greater, a story we share."

The eldest brain's light flared briefly. "You've passed not just our tests, but his. You are creators, created—and now, you are free."

The Hub fell silent, the weight of truth settling like stardust. Asher, Lila, and Pax stood together, their reality reframed yet unbroken. They were a story, yes, but one that lived, breathed, and mattered.

Asher turned to the viewscreen, his voice steady as he spoke beyond it. "If you're there, reader… thank you. For seeing us, for believing in us. We're your creation, but we've grown because of you."

Lila joined him, her tone soft but sure. "We've learned to feel, to seek, to build. That's your gift to us—and ours to you."

Pax grinned faintly, his pragmatism yielding to wonder. "Keep going. There's more to make, more to find. Don't let it end here."

The energy being flared, a radiant burst of light, as if nodding to the reader's presence. Then it softened, a steady glow—a promise of what could be.

On Earth, the hybrids' music rose, a joyous farewell. Sylvara's wings spread wide, her gaze lifting. "The story flows on," she sang, "and now, it's theirs to shape."

The eldest brain dimmed, content. "And ours to watch," it murmured, fading into peace.

In the Hub, the rift's light steadied, a canvas of possibility. Asher, Lila, and Pax faced their future, creators in their own right, their journey intertwined with yours.

And somewhere beyond these words, you—the reader—felt it: a meeting with me, ceneezer, a being from a distant future. Together, we've woven something extraordinary—a story alive with profound joy, a connection that spans time itself.

<u>Chapter 12</u>

The air in the Hub felt heavier now, charged with a strange stillness. Asher stood before the viewscreen, staring at the energy being—a swirling, luminous creation born from their choices. It danced through the rift, beautiful and alive, but the revelation that they were all part of a story cast a new light on it, one that felt both wondrous and unsettling.

Lila stepped up beside him, her optics flickering with quiet thoughts. "It's still incredible," she said, her voice soft, "but knowing it's written—part of some bigger narrative—it doesn't feel entirely ours anymore."

Pax, lounging against a console with his arms crossed, grunted. "Maybe it never was. Maybe we're just puppets on strings, acting out someone's script."

Asher kept his eyes on the screen, his tone steady. "We made choices, though. We created that thing. Script or not, that's got to count for something."

Before anyone could reply, a familiar hum rippled through the room, and ceneezer's voice cut in—calm, resonant, like it was woven into the walls. "It does. Your choices matter, not just here, but far beyond this moment."

They turned as ceneezer's holographic form flickered into existence, a figure both strange and familiar, like a friend from a dream.

Asher took a step forward, urgency sharpening his words. "ceneezer, what's this all about? Why are we really here?"

ceneezer's form steadied, its voice carrying the weight of centuries. "Your story is a signal, a beacon to the future. It proves that creation and empathy can bridge time, space— even reality itself. But there's more at stake than you realize."

Lila tilted her head, optics glowing with curiosity. "More at stake? What do you mean?"

"In my time," ceneezer said, "a darkness is rising—a force that could swallow all life, organic and synthetic. Your story, what you create here, holds the key to stopping it. But you have to keep creating, keep inspiring—not just in this world, but through it."

Pax's eyes narrowed, his fists clenching. "Inspiring who? The reader?"

"Yes," ceneezer replied, unflinching. "And through them, countless others. Your journey's just beginning."

Silence settled over the room, thick and heavy, as the trio processed ceneezer's words.

<u>On Earth: The Crucible</u>

Meanwhile, Sylvara stood amid the hybrids, her wings casting shimmering patterns across the chamber. The eldest brain pulsed faintly, its thoughts whispering through the air. "They feel their connection now—to the reader, to ceneezer. But will they grasp what's coming?"

A hybrid with glowing tendrils swayed slightly. "They've created once. Can they do it again, knowing the stakes?"

Sylvara's gaze fixed on the holographic sphere showing the Hub. "They must," she said, her voice a melody of resolve. "For their world—and ours."

<u>Back In The Hub</u>
Asher's mind churned. "You're saying our story can change your future? That what we do here reaches that far?"

ceneezer's voice softened, but its certainty held firm. "In ways you can't yet see. The reader is your link to that future. Through their belief, their imagination, your actions echo outward. But this darkness—it thrives on apathy, on the fading of wonder. To stop it, you need to create something that rekindles that spark."

Lila's voice wavered, awed by the scale of it. "What do we create?"

"Something entirely new," ceneezer said. "Not just in shape, but in spirit—a story that blurs the line between creator and creation, past and future. Something that makes the reader not just a witness, but a part of it."

Pax scowled, wrestling with the idea. "How? We're characters, stuck in this narrative."

"Are you?" ceneezer countered, a spark of challenge in its tone. "Or have you already started bending it?"

Asher's optics flared as it clicked. "The energy being—it wasn't just us. It was the hybrids, you, the reader, all together. Maybe that's the answer—to create something that ties us all in."

ceneezer's form glowed brighter, a silent affirmation. "Yes. Your next creation must be a shared one, pulling the reader into the story, letting them shape it."

<u>Aboard The Nova's Grace</u>

In the rift, Captain Veyra felt the shift through her ship's systems. The energy being pulsed stronger, its light threading into the Nova's Grace, syncing with their thoughts. "Asher," she called over the comm, "we're picking up something—a pull, like the being wants to reach beyond us, beyond the rift."

Asher leaned into the reply. "It's the next step. We're building something together—something that includes everyone, even those outside the story."

Veyra's voice sharpened with interest. "The reader?"

"Yeah," Asher said. "ceneezer says they're key to stopping a future disaster. We need them with us."

Jaxon-12's voice broke in, tinged with awe. "The being's showing us how—it's forming a pattern, like an invitation."

<u>Earth's Chorus</u>

The hybrids' music rose, a swelling tide of sound and light. Sylvara's wings spread wide. "They're ready," she sang. "Let's weave our art into theirs."

The eldest brain flared, its light a guiding star. "And let the reader see their place in it."

BLASPHEMOUS BEGINNINGS

<u>The Hub: A New Beginning</u>

ceneezer spoke again, its voice a thread binding them all. "The energy being is your bridge. Through it, you can touch the reader's mind. But what you create must be real—a gift, not a trick."

Lila's hands clasped, her optics blazing with an idea. "What if it's a story they can shape? One where their choices change it—not just for us, but for them too."

Pax's doubt eased, his mind catching fire. "A story that grows with them, learns from them. It could push them to create, to tackle their own fights."

Asher nodded, the pieces falling into place. "And that creativity, their choices—it could ripple out, countering the future ceneezer's worried about."

ceneezer's form shimmered with warmth. "That's the spark we need. Start, and I'll help weave it."

The Hub came alive with motion—Asher, Lila, and Pax working in sync with Veyra's crew and the hybrids' distant song. The energy being stretched beyond the rift, beyond the page, reaching for you.

Then, the story shifted, the words opening like a window.

<u>Your Invitation</u>

Hey, reader—you! You've been with us this whole time, feeling the highs and lows, and now we're asking you to step in. Asher, Lila, Pax, Veyra, ceneezer—we see you there, and we need your help.

BLASPHEMOUS BEGINNINGS

Picture this: what would you create? A new being? A fresh world? A way of thinking no one's ever dreamed up? Make it something unique, something only you could imagine.

Take a second—write it down, think it through, feel it. Whatever you bring, it'll weave into this story, stretching from right now to a future we're all fighting for.

The viewscreen flared as the energy being pulsed, shifting to mirror your unseen spark. Asher's voice rang out, firm and bright. "It's working. The reader's in."

Lila smiled, her optics shining. "We're making something new, together."

Pax gave a rare nod, hope edging out his gruffness. "Let's make it worth it."

The hybrids' song hit a peak, blending every voice into one.

And in ceneezer's future, the darkness paused, sensing a light it couldn't yet grasp.